# Cannibals

# Cannibals

SHINYA TANAKA

*Translated by Kalau Almony*

Honford
Star

This translation first published by Honford Star 2024

Honford Star Ltd.
Profolk, Bank Chambers
Stockport
SK1 1AR
honfordstar.com

Originally published in Japanese as TOMOGUI
© 2012 Shinya Tanaka / CTB Inc.
All rights reserved
English translation rights arranged with CTB Inc. through
Japan UNI Agency, Inc., Tokyo.
English translation copyright © 2024 Kalau Almony

ISBN (paperback): 978-1-915829-09-2
ISBN (ebook): 978-1-915829-10-8
A catalogue record for this book is available from the British Library.

Printed and bound in Paju, South Korea
Cover design by Jun Kawana
Typeset by Honford Star
Cover paper: 250 gsm Vent Nouveau by TAKEO, Japan
Endleaves: 116 gsm NT Rasha by TAKEO, Japan


1 3 5 7 9 10 8 6 4 2

IN JULY OF 1989, the sixty-third year of the Showa era, on the day he turned seventeen, Shinogaki Toma did not go home at the end of the day's lessons. Instead, he headed straight to Aida Chigusa's house. Chigusa was a year older than him and went to a different high school. They both, however, lived in the same area, the riverside, and their homes were less than a three-minute walk apart.

Toma got off the bus on the freeway and walked down a narrow road bordered by old homes and buildings filled with rented shops and offices until he reached the river, which he then walked along, following its current. The river was about ten meters across. It was low tide and the yellow earth of the riverbed was visible through the shallow water. Stones of all shapes and sizes; a broken bicycle that looked as though even if someone tried to ride it, it could do nothing but turn right for eternity; a black umbrella whose broken frame thrust out of the water like the mast of a ship; a tinplated bucket which, except for the bright crimson handle, was rusted into a shapeless heap; wooden fencing; plastic bags swollen with sand—these and other pieces of trash filled the river. Schools of young mullet swam through the water. The mud of the riverbank was covered in birds' footprints that looked like swarms of giant spiders and pocked with piles of black slime in the spots where the birds had been digging for food with their beaks. Green algae clung to both the garbage in the river and the riverbank itself. The algae were evidence of the tide, proof that this was not fresh water. All of these things mingled with the rising sea, and what was left by the receding tide gave the river shape as they waited for the sea to come again.

Then came the smell. The riverside's sewage system had not yet been completed. Houses did have indoor plumbing and flush toilets; however, the sewage was carried directly to the river. It had been decided that homeowners would shoulder some part of the cost of connecting each house's sewage system to the main line, and construction was slated for next spring, so the intense stench of summer would also end this year.

The smell was awful, and, what was worse, it meant home and his father. Whenever Toma smelled this odor, he felt as though he had arrived back home. This was not a joyous feeling, but nor was it an entirely unbearable one. Just as Toma simply accepted the river as the river and the bridge as the bridge, he accepted the feeling of arriving home as what it always was. Yet Toma also suspected that today might actually be the first time he noticed this feeling of what it was to come home.

Toma cut a path through the stagnant stink as he walked. When the tide was coming in, the smell of the ocean mingled with the smell of the river; the air vibrated and clung. A skinny red dog tied to the gutter of a warehouse facing the road ran to the end of its chain and started barking. Toma passed by a swarm of mosquitos.

He stopped in front of the fish shop. There were no customers. His eyes met those of Jinko-san, his mother. She was wearing her black apron and gutting a fish.

"Heading home?"

"Yeah."

"Today's your birthday."

"Yeah."

"Want a Coke?"

"I'm good."

"All right then. Come stop by soon."

Jinko-san's right hand was out of sight, hidden behind the glass case full of fish. Diagonal from the fish shop, on the other side of the river, was an apartment building with heavy-looking, iron-framed windows, and there, sitting straight on the ground near a corner of that building, was a woman dressed in clothes so white and thin that one could just barely tell they were not her underwear. She was only about forty, but she looked as though she had been waiting like that for a man to return since before there was war.

Toma crossed the bridge. From what looked like a white balloon tied to the handrail rose a head; the balloon transformed into a heron and took flight. Someone must've been doing laundry. Water full of bubbles flowed out of an earthen pipe.

Jinko-san was Toma's birth mother, and a woman called Kotoko-san lived with him and his father, Madoka.

Jinko-san the fishmonger was near sixty, and her right arm from the wrist down was gone. During the war she had got pinned under her burning, collapsed house in an air raid. They went and got the whole riverside all at once, it was an ocean of fire, I traded one hand to keep my life, Toma had heard her say once. That was the only time he had heard Jinko-san talk about how she had lost her right hand. Once was more than enough. The skin from her wrist up to near the elbow was still scarred with burns shaped like the brilliant waves of flame that had incinerated the riverside.

*Cannibals*

About three years after the war, Jinko-san met a man whom she thought she would marry. One day that man's mother said, She better not give birth to a kid with no hand, and Jinko-san, moving so quickly she never gave the man a chance to intervene, forced open his mother's mouth with her left hand, which at that time could move with the same precision of her once dominant hand, and shoved in the tip of her right arm. Apparently she asked, perfectly calm, You want me to shove that tongue down to your stomach? Though the man begged her for forgiveness and pleaded for her to still marry him, she of course never saw him again. Because Jinko-san had lost both her parents in the war, she relied on other relatives to get by for a while and then wound up living and working at the fishmonger's. Unlike the areas near the seaside or the train station, the riverside was left behind by most postwar development, and the people who had gathered there, intending only to temporarily avoid dire poverty, ended up stuck. It was that sort of backwater. One of those men who stayed was Madoka. He was ten years younger than Jinko-san, but the two met at the hilltop shrine overlooking the riverside at the annual summer festival, started dating, and then married. Jinko-san had apparently never even considered the possibility that another man who wanted to marry an old woman with no hand would ever appear. Only after moving to the Shinogaki home, crossing the bridge every day to go to work at the fish shop, did she discover that Toma's father was involved with a slew of other women and that during sex he grew violent. When Jinko-san was pregnant, this tendency to violence receded, but in its place he spent even more time philandering. A year after Toma was born, Madoka started hitting her again, so she left without bothering to get a divorce and began living alone in the fish shop, which she had already taken over completely from the previous owner. Her reason for not taking her son was a simple one: You're that man's seed, aren't you? When she left, Toma's younger brother or sister was already growing inside her, but it was never born. I was past forty so I figured it'd be my last child, but one child from that man was plenty, I went and had 'em go scrape it out of me at the hospital, she said. As he grew up and began comparing himself to his classmates, Toma did realize it was quite strange to be living apart from his mother, but he could always cross the river and visit her at the fish shop, so he never considered moving in with her.

Kotoko-san, who worked near the seaside in one of the many bars in the area, moved into the Shinogaki home about a year ago. While she was not exactly beautiful, she was well endowed in the chest and rear, and her skin made her look young for a thirty-five-year-old. Toma's father, who liked to

*Cannibals*

frequent bars but could not hold his alcohol, had gone repeatedly to the bar she worked at until he managed to seduce her. Sometimes there would be bruises around Kotoko-san's cheeks and eyes. It seemed Toma's father did not hit her until they started living together. When Toma asked, Why don't you break up with him? You scared of him? she laughed and responded, He tells me I got a great body, and when he hits me he says it gets even more better. To Toma she looked like an incredibly stupid woman.

Even after Kotoko-san moved in, Toma's father continued to walk the town. In particular, his affair with the woman from the apartment building never seemed to end. The entrance to her apartment was on the side of the building facing away from the river, so from the fish shop you could not see him arriving, but if the woman was not there sitting on the corner at the back of the building, that was proof that either Toma's father or some other man was there.

Since Toma was young, his father had been part of some sort of business Toma did not really understand. All sorts of calls came to the house, as did people who, no matter how you looked at them, did not look like normal businessmen. He often went out on business as well. There was a truck, the owner of which was unclear, always parked in the garage, and in the back of it Toma would sometimes find piled metal assemblages that were probably used as parts for some sort of machine, or tons of one-liter cans so rusted they looked as though they would disintegrate any minute, sometimes stones so dusty they looked like they had just been mined from some mountain, TVs and sewing machines that could probably never be used again, gas-powered water-heaters, and sometimes cardboard boxes stuffed with brand-new collected editions of literary works. It seemed his father was in the business of buying or selling, or temporarily holding on to, and occasionally disposing of, this wide range of products. Once, someone had pulled back the tarp covering the bed of the truck from the inside, and a woman wearing heavy makeup peeked out and then hid back under. Toma had approached the truck quietly; he heard them speaking in a language that was not Japanese or English, and while he was not sure, it was probably not Chinese or Korean either. Their voices were monotonous and sweet and had a warmth to them, like notes from an instrument of shape and material Toma could not imagine.

At their earliest, Chigusa's parents came home just before six. Birthday sex was rushed as always. At least things ended without catastrophe, unlike their first time, when upon touching Toma's erect penis to put on a condom, he immediately came.

*Cannibals*

They had known each other since they were young, but spring of this year Toma realized that he was doing something, saying something, in front of Chigusa. Afterwards, he had to ask her what he had done.

"You looked like you wanted to touch your dick, your hand was moving around all dangerous, and you said you'd give me the right to end things whenever I like, so I should go out with you."

They had promised to save what would be the first time for both of them for Toma's birthday, just before summer vacation, but of course they broke that promise in less than a month. At first, they had kept count of how many times they did it, but they no longer knew how many times today would make it.

"Is this okay?"

"What? It wasn't good for you?"

"It was good. But I wonder if it's okay to do it like this."

"That's what you were thinking about while we did it?"

"Not while, but once we're done, I start thinking I'm just like my dad. I just like sex."

"Mā-kun, you don't hit me."

"It's too late if I realize I'm like him after I hit you."

"You're never gonna hit me. But you probably should ask yourself if it's okay to keep doing it this way."

"What do you mean?"

"Maybe it feels good for you, but for me it just hurts."

Toma did not know what to say. He thought about his father and the bruises his father gave Kotoko-san.

They left the Aida house and went to the shrine. The shrine was on the west side of the river, the same side as the fish shop, up on the same hill as the elementary and junior high schools. They had just had their fill of sex and did not feel like going all the way to the arcade on the other side of the highway just to waste money, so they did as they always did since they were children when they had spare time and went to the shrine without any intention to pray. At the torii at the top of the stone stairs, Toma asked, just to check, "Not today, right?"

"No, not today."

The old folks always said that when women were having their period, they had to walk around the torii. Jinko-san, who prayed at the shrine every day, had mentioned to him about half a year ago, I'm done with that, I'm free.

The children had been mindlessly running around the shrine grounds and playing a game where they throw stones against other stones to protect their territory, just as Toma and his friends did when he was in elementary school, but when they saw Toma and Chigusa they started making a scene.

"Mā-kun and Chigusa-san are dating!"

*Cannibals*

Though there was still ample evening light, the herd of little bodies seemed to be wrapped in darkness. Toma suddenly felt afraid; he stared at their game, knowing he would never play it again.

Though she had not planned to, Chigusa rang the bell and clapped her hands together in front of the shrine, and afterwards, turning around to look down at the river, said, "And there's the slit today, too."

It was Toma's father who had told them that the river was a woman's slit. Unlike the bit about going around the torii during a period, this pearl was his father's alone. The upper part of the river ran underground, beneath the street of a residential area, and the lower part was covered by the highway, so only for the approximately two-hundred meters that it flowed through the riverside was the river visible as it made its way to the ocean, and from the shrine on the hill, with the river's path bordered by willow trees and their drooping leaves and branches, depending on how you looked at it, it was not impossible to see what Toma's father was talking about. Compared to the ones on the other side of the river around the highway, the houses in the riverside, even the two-story ones, were short like they had been squashed, and though each and every one was constructed differently, they were all alike in their age. Unlike the river, time flowed in every direction and looked as though it could be gone around or crossed over, or in some cases even stopped or killed, if someone did not like the way it was moving. Yet having surrendered itself without any plan or preparation to time's gradual advance, the riverside had, without realizing it, wound up moving backwards, the residents confusing the flow of time with the flow of the river.

"I wonder if River Slit-san ever feels pain."

"Does it hurt that much?"

"Don't worry about it. Sometime soon."

What would happen sometime soon, Toma could not imagine. The green of the willows watched over the river slit.

"You better stop calling the river a slit."

"I know. But your dad's got such a way with words."

"Calling the river a slit. That's so stupid. Screw the river. As long as we live in a place like this, it doesn't matter, whatever we do. No matter how hard we try, in the end it all just gets swallowed up by the river."

"Hey, don't make like that. Mā-kun, you're not the river, but you still find your way inside me."

"Yeah, and that's why I'm just like my dad, right? I can't do anything but fuck. Here, by this river, there's nothing worth doing except that."

"When you were little you used to go fishing."

*Cannibals*

Now, Toma only fished for unagi.

"Those kids back there, they don't even really go in the river anymore. But back when we were little, the river was even more dirtier, but the fish were big."

"You sure you weren't just smaller, Mā-kun?"

A heron, its neck pulled back in a somehow lascivious pose, flew past them, almost grazing the hill as it went, and landed amidst the willows.

"Wanna come over? Eat dinner?"

Toma had not invited Chigusa over since they started going out.

"I'm gonna go home. I'm tired. And ..." Chigusa placed her hand beneath her bellybutton. "It's still a little ..."

"It hurts?"

"Not as much as when we were doing it."

"I guess I'm just no good at all, ay."

"No, I don't think that's true. It's just gonna take a little experience and some hard work. You know?"

Experience sounded to Toma like it meant hitting Chigusa, and he went silent.


"You're late. Where were you?"

Toma entered his house, ignored his father who was laying in the tatami room sticking his head out through the door, walked carefully around the head of thinning, white hair looking up at him, and made for upstairs.

"Come on, you can't answer your father?"

He was not drunk, and no matter how rough his tone when scolding Toma, he would never raise a hand to him. Toma had never been struck by his father.

Kotoko-san peeked out of the kitchen and said, "Welcome home. Mā-kun, were you on a date?"

Toma paused on the stairs to glare at Kotoko-san before climbing the rest of the way up.

His father's voice chased after him. "Toma, you got a girl?"

Toma could hear Kotoko-san answer. "He does. My customer said he saw them together. Him and Chigusa-chan, the Aidas' girl."

While Toma was changing from his school uniform into a T-shirt and shorts, he heard his father from downstairs say, "Aw, shit. I wanna do it with one young girl again," and then, "I'm gonna be late tonight," before walking off in his geta.

The thick piece of meat Kotoko-san had brought out for dinner was grilled a deep brown and jiggled just from her placing the plate on the table. On the side she had prepared grilled potatoes and boiled string beans.

"Since it's your birthday, he went all out with meat and a cake. Your dad did."

*Cannibals*

Kotoko's hair was pulled back, but a loose strand was stuck to her bruised cheek. Toma remembered Chigusa saying, You're never gonna hit me, but that recollection was soon erased by Kotoko-san's arms and her ample chest filling out her short-sleeved shirt. Toma pounded on his plate with his knife and fork as he ate his meat.

After dinner, Kotoko-san went to work. Toma washed the greasy plates. Bugs chirped under the sink.

Toma was not sure if he woke up because he wanted to go to the bathroom or because he sensed the commotion downstairs. He did not know when his father, who had said he would be late, had actually come home. It was five in the morning. From the top of the stairs, moving just his eyes, Toma peeked into the living room lit only by a single, small bulb. It was not the first time he had seen this. His small father was buried in Kotoko-san's voluptuous body, and the mass of their flesh moved frustrated but unceasing, as though savoring the lack of freedom. His father released a short, sharp wail, and Kotoko-san panted loudly. Eventually, a division formed between the two merged bodies. His father leaned his torso back as he continued to thrust his hips, grabbed Kotoko-san by the hair, and slapped her cheek with his other hand. Kotoko-san's gasp followed the fleshy noise, and as if in response, his father's movements grew faster. He placed both hands on Kotoko-san's neck and began to strangle her. His hips pumped up and down mechanically; he looked up to the ceiling and thrust, made a noise like water being sucked through a small hole, froze, and collapsed, breathing heavily. He stood up and said, "Oh my," softly as though he had just woken from a nap.

When is the next time I'll see this, Toma wondered. From between the downstairs ceiling and the handrail of the stairs he could see Kotoko-san, her body stretched out as though all her joints had been pulled out of place, and the lower half of his father, probably staring down at her. His reddish-brown penis, still erect and standing perfectly horizontal, trembled with the rhythm of his breathing.

"We start in the evening. You go ahead. Don't wait up. You can start without me. Use the nail hooks."

It would be their first time unagi fishing since Toma's summer break began. His father handed out orders but was laying on the tatami, pulling out his nose hairs.

Jinko-san threw the bones and skin of the fish she cleaned straight into the river, so unagi would gather in front of the fish shop. Only recently did Toma come to realize how unhygienic and dangerous it was for his father to eat the unagi they

*Cannibals*

would catch in that river pumped full of sewage. There was no one else in the riverside who would touch the stuff, and Toma himself had never eaten the unagi they caught.

Before going fishing, Toma went to Chigusa's house and they had sex. Both of her parents worked, so it was far safer than Toma's house, where no one could ever predict when his father would be home or not. Just before entering Chigusa, Toma stood up and looked at his organ. It pointed slightly upward. Chigusa's whole body was tense. She let out a deep sigh and asked, "What's wrong? What you thinking?"

Still looking at his penis, Toma responded, "Tonight, I'm gonna go fishing. Unagi. That's all."

Toma inserted himself slowly, and did his best to be soft, to move not like a machine but the gentle back and forth of waves on the shore. It did not feel as good as when he rushed like always. Chigusa was clearly still in pain.

Toma returned home that evening and his father was gone.

"Where'd he go?" he asked Kotoko-san, who was taking down the laundry.

"He's snooping."

"Snooping? For what?"

"There's this customer at my bar. A young guy. Apparently, your dad's been going to the bar and other shops and places trying to find out if we're together."

Toma went down into the garden with an empty instant coffee jar to search for earthworms.

"Is it true?"

"Hm? What? I mean, which one you talking about? His snooping around, or whether I've got someone else?"

"Yeah, that."

"I can't believe it. Even Mā-kun doubts me," she said with a laugh.

Toma lifted up a pot without a plant in it. It had not rained recently, and the soil beneath the pot, which was usually damp, had dried out completely. There were just a few pill bugs, so he went to check by the hole that connects to the river, where the hose from the washing machine goes. There was a thin layer of green moss, which Toma dug up with the lid of the jar. He caught five or six worms. If that was not enough, he would ask Jinko-san for her leftovers from the fish shop.

"Should I pack you a bento?"

"Don't worry about it. I'm gonna eat at the shop. Sorry."

"You don't need to apologize."

When he stepped outside, he felt a little faint. He had spent almost every day with Chigusa. In the evening sky, the lights were on in the apartments next to the highway beyond the willow-lined riverside.

As he walked along the riverbank, the bugs in the grass

*Cannibals*

covering the willow roots would stop their crying when he passed and then start again immediately behind him. He was surprised at how loud the insects were already, and as he watched the asphalt path appear from the darkness one step in front of him at a time and then vanish behind him, Toma began to feel as though not just this summer, but the shape of the riverside and its people and even time were being carried away. It was like when he saw the children at the shrine on his birthday, in the darkness that had not yet even arrived. Were there really children in the shrine grounds then? He felt that everything was vanishing into the distance. Yet he also sensed that everything in the riverside had been there since long ago and had existed without changing and would continue on unchanged. The rail of the bridge, which he knew was actually brown with rust, looked to him white like bone. The ocean, now approaching high tide, was heaving its way into the slit-river. Low waves pulled in the evening light and climbed up the revetment, swelling and contracting to fit themselves deftly into its unevenness. What looked like a mullet or young sea bass jumped from the water and shone. The sound was solid but quiet. Toma felt himself enveloped in the mingling smells of sea and sewage as the heavy, hot night seeped into his body. He wiped his neck with his hand. His sweat felt like melted skin.

He saw the lights of the fish shop. The shop was already closed, but when they went night fishing, Jinko-san would keep the lights on. His dad was not there. Jinko-san was standing in front of her cutting board. She said, "He stuck his head in a second ago. I don't know where he went, but he left."

The woman was sitting on the corner of the apartment building across the river, wearing her white clothes, fanning herself.

"I wish he wouldn't boss me around if he was never gonna come anyway."

When he went fishing here with his father, he could be together with both of his parents, so Toma always joined his father when asked.

Jinko-san was still wearing her work clothes. The end of her right arm was wrapped in a rag, over which her prosthetic was attached. The prosthetic was not shaped like a hand; it was a cylinder of long, thin stainless-steel rods. Jinko-san would slide the narrower center of that cylinder over the rag on her arm and then secure it in place with a leather belt wrapped around the outside. It looked as if her arm from the elbow down was caught in a long, thin metal cage. The end of the prosthetic was fitted with nonstick rubber. She would use that to hold down fish on the cutting board while with the knife in her left hand she could descale them and open their bellies. Only when she cleaned unagi did she hold the fish directly with her metal talons so as to make sure they did not slip. She would loosen the screws and remove the rubber stopper. When she did that, her hand would make a strange *pop*.

This bizarre and tragic looking right hand of hers, this hand that could be called a kind of machine, was Toma's father's doing. He had heard Jinko-san complaining that the prosthetic the hospital recommended her, one that looked like a hand, was no good for her day-to-day work, so he talked to the owner of a small factory operating in the riverside at the time that processed sheet metal and steel frames and had this made before they got married. The original one broke within two years, so they had a new one made after reflecting on the weak points of the original, and they changed parts and had new ones made a few times since then. After the factory shut down, Jinko-san did not know where to take her hand for repairs. She would take it to the bicycle shop and the watchmaker and the glasses shop in the shopping district on the other side of the river, or she would treat it herself with WD-40 and nurse the thing into use, but it was almost time to retire it. She was thinking that when the current one broke, she would just make do with one of those slippery prosthetics that are no good for cleaning fish and either go all out and hire someone or pass the shop along to someone else. Toma was one of the contenders.

Upon seeing her son, Jinko-san had taken out another fish and placed it on her old cutting board, which was worn down in the center. Toma took the two fishing poles leaning against the wall and the tackle box next to them out of the shop. He leaned one pole against the fence on the revetment and took the other in his hands and checked the reel. He attached a clip-on bell to the end of the rod so he could tell in the darkness if he had a bite. He slid the fishing line through the hole in the center of a sinker, so worn from use that he could no longer make out the faded number on the weight's surface. He attached the swivel to the line and tied the leader to that. On one pole he used the hook for unagi that he had bought at the fishing supply shop, and on the other he attached the nail hook, as his father had instructed.

To make a nail hook, first you have to cut off the head of the nail, then file it down until it is as sharp as the other side. Next you file the middle to make a small indent, and smooth it down with sandpaper. To use it, you tie the fishing line around the indentation in the middle, and put one worm on each side. If the unagi gets hooked properly when it bites, the nail will make a horizontal line in the fish's mouth and get lodged into both of its sides. If done right, there is no

*Cannibals*

chance the fish will break free. Toma had used this nail hook many times, but he still had not mastered it. Either he did not sharpen the flat side enough, or he did not file the spot where you tie on the hook enough and damaged his leader, or he failed in hooking the fish when he did get a bite.

Toma leaned the rods against the fence and waited inside the fish shop for a bite. The smell of the incoming tide was gradually winning out over the smell of sewage. The tide did not matter too much when night fishing, but still he felt that just the fact that there was lots of water meant he would catch a big one.

The lights of the fish shop were growing more and more noticeable. There was no wind. The leaves of the hydrangeas growing around the rails stood like the spines on the back of a large reptile. They were still. The night seemed ready to freeze along with time itself. Only the tips of the two fishing rods, which looked thinner than they did in the light, moved, bobbing up and down with the gentle motion of the rising tide. Not enough for either bell to ring.

"How's this?"

Jinko-san brought Toma a bowl. There was rice topped with mackerel and sardines she had smashed with her knife, along with green onion. It smelt of shoyu. On one side of the bowl were two slices of pickled eggplant. Toma mixed it with his chopsticks and shoveled it into his mouth. Jinko-san threw the fish entrails into the river, and when she was done washing her cutting board and knife, she removed her prosthetic hand, hung it from a hook screwed into a beam, and climbed up into the room behind her shop. Cigarette smoke eventually drifted into the shop, clouding the air slightly.

"Is something wrong?"

At the sound of his mother's voice, Toma recalled the young man that Kotoko-san had mentioned.

"Why? Did Dad say something?"

"He doesn't need to. You can see it in those eyes. They were always trouble, that man's eyes. The other day, on your birthday, he had the same look. Like his blood was boiling."

On his birthday when his father heard about Chigusa from Kotoko-san, he had said he wanted to do it with a young girl one more time and then left before dinner. The next day early in the morning, Toma had seen him with Kotoko-san.

"Can I ask something? Dad, when he stays here, does he hit you?"

The bell rang. Toma put down the bowl and chopsticks and went outside. It was the rod with the nail hook. He worried that he might mess it up, but still Toma picked up the rod. He had a bite so he had to try and set the hook. Thinking the fish might have already swallowed the hook whole, he

*Cannibals*

tried pulling on the rod. Maybe it was caught on something on the riverbed. It would not move. He lowered the rod and then pulled; he tried to reel it in with all his strength, but it still did not budge. Maybe it was just some garbage carried by the tide brushing against the line that rang the bell. He tried to reel it in again and shook the rod slightly. The bell rang with each motion. After several attempts, he felt something peeling off the riverbed and rising, slowly pulling the line away with a sticky force. It was not pulling hard but like it had no choice. It moved in a straight line, but the motion was very dull. Not pulling so much as sinking forever under its own weight. The rod arced steeply under that weight. Toma turned the reel. This was the first time he had ever felt such a solid pull on a nail hook. The gentle flapping of the fan by the woman at the corner of the apartment building came and went from his peripheral vision. Bugs were singing in the leaves of the hydrangeas next to him. A bat passed under the arc of the rod and line.

From the smooth trembling of the river's surface rose a spray of water dyed gold by the light of the fish shop, and in a wild figure-eight dragged twisting by the fishing line came rising up an unagi. Toma watched its whole body get tangled in the line. He carried the eel to his side of the rail with the precision of a crane operator and lowered it onto the ground.

The unagi had about the same girth as the handle of the fishing rod. Maybe because of all the times Toma had tugged on the line, the nail had pierced through both sides of the fish, and one side of its face was torn open. The protruding, narrow lips of the unagi, biting down on the lead, shone dark green. It wriggled feebly, trying to free itself from the line it was tangled in. Toma was excited. He could feel a warmth building in the pit of his stomach. This was partly because he had successfully caught an unagi with a nail hook for the first time, but he could tell it was also from seeing the split and half-collapsed head of the eel.

Toma carried the rod with the catch still on the line into the fish shop. Jinko-san had already reattached her prosthetic hand and placed the unagi, lead and all, in the sink. Loosening the screws of her prosthetic with her left hand, soon came the *pop* and the rubber end came off. She held the eel down gently, not with the full strength she would use when cleaning one, and stroked the wriggling body with her left hand to squeeze out the nail, then threw the eel in a bucket. She immediately filled it with water, covered it with a pot lid turned upside down, and placed a brick on the indented center to weigh it down. She would leave it like this for one night to let it spit up the mud. The contents of its stomach seemed more likely to escape from the gash on its head than from its mouth.

*Cannibals*

The woman had vanished from the corner of the apartment building. Toma could hear faintly the sound of the red dog's chain. Jinko-san returned to the back of the shop and started smoking again. Baiting the nail hook with new worms, Toma cast it back out. He reeled in the other rod and found caught on it a goby not much bigger than the hook itself, dead on the line. As he pulled it off the hook, he ripped open its mouth. He felt a warmth in his body once again. He forced the nail of his thumb into its gill. The shape of its head collapsed steadily under his thumb. The dead flesh put up no resistance. Toma's fever chilled. He threw the fish into the river.

He washed his hands in the sink and returned to his bowl of fish.

"You were saying something earlier. Something about when he stays here?"

After seeing the crushed head of that fish, he could not remember what he had wanted to ask.

"Oh. Never mind. It was nothing."

But Jinko-san continued. "He never stays here no more. He sticks his head in, then goes out. He's not interested in women who aren't women anymore. But Kotoko-san is still probably getting it, unlike me."

Her words sounded terribly cold to Toma, and he turned to look at her, but all that was there was a shadow with a cigarette in its mouth. He could not make out the details of her face.

"If he's with a real woman, he hits them. He can't be a man if he doesn't."

Toma finished eating and poured tea into the bowl, the sides stuck with shoyu and grains of rice, and drank it. Jinko-san offered him her cigarette pack.

"No, thanks."

"You're like him. You don't smoke. What about alcohol?"

"What're you saying? What kinda parent offers their kid cigarettes and booze?"

"Even if I don't offer them to you, one day soon you'll do one or both."

She spoke as though she were hopeful for her son.

The large cat Toma sometimes saw stretched its striped back and sauntered through the shop without making a single sound. It climbed up into the house with Jinko-san and walked towards the back door. From behind the cat looked unnaturally large—it made Toma think that the fish shop must have somehow passed through the cat's body instead of it through the shop. If this shop could pass through that cat, then all the garbage at the bottom of the river and the time stopped in the riverside should be able to pass through it easily as well.

Toma kept his lines out until past nine, but in the end all he

*Cannibals*

caught was the one unagi. His father never showed. The woman across the way never reappeared. He took apart the rigs and returned the rods and tackle box to their original position.

"I'll come get it tomorrow," Toma said, pointing to the bucket with the unagi, and then left the shop.

At home, the lights Kotoko-san had turned on before leaving for the bar were still on, but his father was not home.

His fever had not chilled completely, and a heat still lingered in Toma's body. He splashed himself with cold water in the bath, but the unagi tangled in transparent fishing line would not vanish from his mind. He felt the filth seeping from the gashes in its head flowing into his body. He gripped his penis. He used his fingers, pretending he was shoving himself into the wound on the unagi's head. Suddenly he was hard, and now his penis was the unagi, and the unagi was swimming into its own wounds and flailing, and the crushed head of the unagi and Chigusa and Kotoko-san all appeared in frighteningly rapid succession one after the other then all blurred together, and the blood rushing to fill him spread like a net trying to catch everything, including Toma himself, and Toma tried to break through his own net of blood, and when he thought he had broken it, he was again wrapped in blood, and when he pressed down on the rising rage with his fingers, he saw clearly Kotoko-san being strangled by his father and it was all over.

He washed himself again with cold water. The grey-white drops splattered everywhere melted into the water and ran to the drain, then flowed into the river.

"Morning." Kotoko-san was cheerful. She was finishing breakfast.

"Where's Dad?"

"He left already. Said he had to take care of some things for the festival."

Next month was the shrine's summer festival.

When Toma took out his penis in the bathroom to urinate, it looked nothing like the neck of Kotoko-san he had just seen.

Toma took a seat at the low table, ate the rice he was served, sipped his miso soup with egg, chomped down a skinny shishamo smelt head-first, and finally, scooped a small second serving of rice into his bowl, poured what egg was left in his soup on top, mixed it all together, and ate it. Kotoko-san stacked her own dishes and spoke, entertained, as she put on tea.

"Just now I thought to myself, Mā-kun eats like a child, but actually, I guess your dad is even more childish. The way you two eat is totally backwards."

His father would dump his whole bowl of soup, egg and all, on top of his rice. Toma found the thought of the grains of rice swimming in brown soup disgusting, so he could not eat that way.

*Cannibals*

"But the way you hold your chopsticks when you eat, even the way your mouths move, you're basically identical."

Kotoko-san handed him a cup of tea. On the inside of the elbow of her meaty arm, sweat was collecting. The smell of Kotoko-san's body overcame the steam of the tea, and Toma's breathing quickened. He was surprised to find himself thinking of the crushed head of the unagi, and in an attempt to block out that image, he reached for his teacup. It was hot.

"I've got something I need to say. Your dad said I should be the one to tell you. I'm pregnant. I plan to keep it. I hope that's okay with you."

Toma responded as if directing a complaint to the heat of the tea. "What? What are you saying? Why do you need to ask me that?"

When he stood up, the teacup tumbled across the table, and he could hear Kotoko-san shout in surprise. He walked to the front door without looking back and put on his sandals.

"Where're you going?"

"To pick it up, the unagi. At the fish shop."

Toma felt his aggressive manner of speaking resembled his father's, and again he saw the head of the unagi, but this time overlaid with the reddish-brown penis he saw in the gap between the handrail of the stairs. The blood of the unagi would make its way to Kotoko-san's belly and begin to grow. After it scraped out the child in her stomach, and Kotoko-san's blood and flesh and bones, all of it, it wanted to shove in its organ and fill her. It wanted to rub up against Kotoko-san stretched into the shape of that organ.

Toma strayed from the road to the fish shop and headed to Chigusa's house. When he saw her, without looking at her face and before even holding her, he tried to take off her clothes. Of course he had not brought a condom.

"Stop messing around. Want me to yell?"

"What, you wanna fuck the condom? Don't you like me?"

"Your eyes are different today. I don't like it."

"You scared of getting pregnant? Would you get rid of it? If you were pregnant with my kid?"

"What're you saying? You're not making sense."

She spoke decisively and glared at him, her face frozen in a way Toma had never seen before, but her lips still shone red as though they had forgotten to hide themselves. He grabbed her head with both hands and pulled it towards his crotch saying, "If you don't want it down there, try with your mouth. I don't care whether it's your top or your bottom if I can get it in you."

Chigusa twisted her body like crazy trying to get away from him. Toma moved his hands down to her neck as though he was going to strangle her, all at once his grip tightening,

*Cannibals*

and in the next second, he let go as if his arms were thrown off by their own force.

Before going to the fish shop, he walked back and forth along the river countless times. He had to get his penis, which was pressing up to his stomach, to settle down. The red dog howled. It was having a fit; its eyes were open wide, its tail standing up. The mass of red at the end of that chain, pulling and then letting it go slack, under the pressure of the dry air from days without rain, was going wild; Toma's penis, now partly deflated, seemed ready to rise in response even to the scene the dog was making. Parts of the riverbed that were usually covered no matter how shallow the river got were now showing their faces, and there was no sign of the ocean at all. Toma grabbed the end of a willow branch and tore it off.

The woman was in her apartment sleeping, her head and arms sticking out of her window. He did not see his father. The shutters of the fish shop were up, but the glass case was mostly empty, and the shop itself was dark. His mother's prosthetic was hanging on the beam.

"I came to get the unagi."

Jinko-san was sitting on a chair, smoking, looking out of the shop, her eyes ready to catch, if it were ever to mistakenly wander by in front of her shop, the time that would never come back. She stood and from the silver refrigerator took out a small pot followed by a bottle of Coke, and removed the cap. In the pot was the unagi cut and cooked shiroyaki, without any sauce, and, as always, the grilled liver.

"Tell her she doesn't need to worry when she returns the pot."

Jinko-san always said this when he came to pick up unagi. It was a message for Kotoko-san, who could never return a borrowed pot empty. Toma had felt that Jinko-san considered that sort of polite gesture a personal affront, and only recently did he realize the obvious: that it was just the normal thing to say when passing back and forth a pot. But in this case, maybe a mutually consensual act of perfect politeness could be taken as the perfect snide taunt.

Holding the pot, Toma drank his soda slowly, one sip at a time. When he was still in elementary school and he would come without any particular reason, just to see Jinko-san, she would always ask, How's that? Is it good? but now she lit a fresh cigarette and said, "Something bothering you? You got this frightening look in your eyes."

"What's frightening about them?"

"You got his look in your eyes. I wish …" Jinko-san pointed at her own face. "I wish I made you look a little more like me. But it's too late for that."

Toma burped. "Kotoko-san is pregnant."

Jinko-san exhaled deeply and narrowed her eyes. "Oh,

*Cannibals*

yeah? Then I guess she won't get beat up for a while. That's how it was with me when I was pregnant with you. He just stopped completely. I guess if you don't want to get beat up by that man, you just got to always keep one after another growing in your belly. I just had you, though. When Kotoko-san has her little one, what are you planning to do? What if they tell you to move out?"

"No idea."

"Well, I guess we don't know if the baby's gonna make it or not."

"How can you say that?"

Jinko-san slowly stubbed out her cigarette in the ash tray.

"Ay, you really want for that baby to be born? I think one person carrying on that man's blood, just you, is plenty. That's the way it is. Think about it. He's always with some girl somewhere, but in the end, you were the only one who was born and grew up. I guess I'm just about the only woman who could bear that man's child."

"You could have had one other one." Toma had intended to speak forcefully, but his voice quivered.

"If I had that child, it would be that man's. Since I got it taken out of me, it stayed mine. With you, I gave birth thinking you were all mine, and as much as it hurts, I have to admit, you wound up being both of ours."

Toma placed the empty Coke bottle on the corner of Jinko-san's cutting board and thanked her for the drink.

"Hey, I heard about Aida Chigusa."

Toma was about to leave the fish shop, but instead he asked, "From who?"

"No one in particular. I can't remember every person and what rumors they bring into this shop. Anyway, couldn't you find a prettier girl." Jinko-san pointed at the pot and added, "And you don't eat that. Tell Kotoko-san not to touch it either."

This was another of Jinko-san's unchanging lines. Toma nodded and left the shop. From behind him, Jinko-san added, "The festival's coming up, so you better avoid anything dirty."

The woman, still asleep in her apartment, was so motionless she appeared dead. On the wall was a single kumazemi cicada. It was not making any noise. The woman would never know that cicada was right next to her while she slept. Toma had no intention of telling her about it. It was as if that cicada had never stopped there. And if that was the case, Toma felt, looking at that woman and that cicada at the same time is a sort of lie. Yet still that red dog was howling. Its teeth were small and white.

Since there was unagi, his dad returned before lunch. When Kotoko-san asked, "What should I do with this?" he said, "It's fine the way it is."

*Cannibals*

"No need to heat it up?"

"I said it's fine the way it is. With ginger and shoyu."

Kotoko-san brought the unagi shiroyaki and three servings of somen noodles to the table along with grated ginger. Toma reached for the ginger quickly, before his father could take it all, and mixed it in with the dipping sauce for his noodles.

His father picked up the roasted liver with his fingers, rolling it around on his tongue like a hard candy before chomping into and then swallowing it. He heaped ginger on top of the cold shiroyaki, then poured shoyu on top of that, spreading the mixture out until it hid the flesh of the eel. Picking up a piece, he shoved the whole thing in his mouth so the ginger would not slip off. Toma had never eaten eel, so he did not even know what it tasted like.

"You're not gonna eat any? You don't wanna try? How lame. Just eat it with ginger, then it doesn't smell."

Toma's father looked his happiest when he was eating unagi. He had a mouthful of somen, but then forced another piece of unagi into his mouth as though the noodles were not satisfying to him. After finishing the rest of the eel's body, at last, he sucked on the head, which Jinko-san always kept attached. He took it from his mouth, checked where there was still meat, and sucked on it again. He repeated this process, and each time he took the long, skinny head from his mouth, more and more of its flesh was stripped away, and it shone faintly with saliva. His father never noticed the wound Toma made when reeling the fish in.

"I got that one with the nail hook."

"Oh. This your first?"

"Yeah."

"Congratulations. Oh no. Why didn't you try some? It was your first catch."

His pale face loosened into a laugh. Maybe he was in a good mood because Kotoko-san was pregnant.

"Jinko-san said not to worry when you return the pot."

Kotoko-san nodded twice silently, slurping her noodles.

July turned to August, but the rain still had not come. When the tide was out, it was obvious how drastically the amount of water coming from upstream had decreased. The mud on the riverside dried out, and the sea slaters somehow endured the hot, heavy, and unmoving air by passing the time in the spaces between rocks in the revetment and the inside of pipes. Herons stopped by the river, but it seemed they were unable to catch much and would always fly off soon after landing. The rats panicked and rushed across the river, as if surprised by how little water there was. An enormous dragonfly as big as a toy model landed on the handle of a broken bicycle pro-truding from the surface of the water, and the way it shook its wings and took off made it truly seem as though it must have been artificial. When the tide came in, it peeled the dried mud off the riverbank, which then floated up, dissolved into the water, and eventually clouded up the ocean water near the mouth of the river, where the tide ran against its current.

Toma could not see Chigusa. She picked up the phone once when he called, but then Toma said, You don't need to forgive me for choking you, but can't we just fuck? I promise I'll make sure it doesn't hurt this time, so she replied simply, Fuck off and die already, and then hung up. Having squandered his last chance, Toma wound up washing his semen down the drain of his bath and into the river every day. It was the place where he was least likely to be bothered by his father or Kotoko-san, and he was as naked as when he had sex, but Chigusa was not there.

As Jinko-san had predicted, Toma's father stopped hitting Kotoko-san, and in fact, it looked as though he had a hard time even approaching her. It makes me kinda sick to hear we know exactly when she's due, he said, and he would give her side-eye glances and hang his head as though he felt guilty for something. Toma wondered if he was sorry for hitting her. He felt as though he was watching his father when his own mother was pregnant with him, but he also could not forget the other thing Jinko-san had said. Would his father kick him out of the house after Kotoko-san's baby was born? He had no intention of living at the fish shop. He sensed that if it came to that he would not just leave the house—he would have to leave the riverside. Up until now, Toma had not really considered what would happen after he graduated from high school. He had not even really decided whether to work or go to college. But both options, continuing to study, which he did not particularly enjoy, and clinging to the riverside and spending his whole life working there like his father and Jinko-san, were unappealing. If he was kicked out by his father, he could imagine going somewhere else. If he was going to leave, Chigusa would go with him. But when he was with Chigusa, he cared more about having sex than thinking about their future together. Once Toma realized that, the future he was struggling to imagine vanished in an instant. Whether he hit Chigusa or not, he wanted to have sex with her.

As Obon approached, there was still no sign of rain, not even in the weather forecast, and the roads, the houses, the bridge, the willows, the barking of the red dog, even time, unclear whether it was moving forward or not, seemed ready to collapse from heat and melt. The herons with their bent, overheated necks seemed as though they might evaporate into the sky at any second. The big striped cat expanded and

*Cannibals*

shrank each time it coughed from choking on the burnt air. The eyes of the woman in the apartment were unnaturally clear. She must have been watching a different life, one she had never before seen even in her dreams, pass her by.

The stagnant riverside time passed as expected, and apparently the city had, because of the great number of complaints from other areas about the smell, settled on trying to find a quick solution to getting sewer pipes installed, even if it meant the city would have to pay significantly more for the project in order to defray part of the expected homeowners' contributions, but despite this the residents of the riverside were not particularly excited to hear that they would be saving money on new sewer pipes, and Toma's father continued to go to the apartment, and to other places, and continued his tireless search for Kotoko-san's other man, who may or may not have existed, and men besides Toma's father tried desperately to hold down the bloated time which they had no hope of ever actually catching and ripping apart—they made excuses to skip work and watch the high school baseball players at the Koshien National Tournament, whose only point of similarity with the people living in the riverside was that they were also roasting in the heat and the light, and they made very little effort to try and leave their homes. The backs of the sea slaters coming and going in the cracks of the revetment, bereft of even the moisture of a summer squall, had grown white and dusty.

Toma went to return the pot to the fish shop. In it were beans Kotoko-san had boiled brown with wakame stems.

Just as Toma noticed that the woman was not on the corner of her apartment building, she came out of the fish shop. The pointed heads of the scabbard fish protruding from the newspaper they were wrapped in were ready to rip apart the clear plastic bag she held. Blood was pooling in the corner of the bag. Their eyes met; the woman paused, tilted her head to the side, then bowed with her body still in that strange pose. Toma entered the fish shop without acknowledging her.

"Kotoko-san said thank you for the pot and sorry it took so long to get it back to you." Toma placed it on the edge of Jinko-san's cutting board.

"Yeah."

Jinko-san nodded slightly and then picked up the pot to put it away. She immediately noticed the weight of it, muttered, "Oh my" under her breath and frowned, her eyebrows twisting slightly. She placed the pot down on the glass case, and after removing the lid to check its contents, said with a slight bow and her hands together as if in prayer, "Tell her thank you."

Toma could not see Chigusa and he had not touched his

*Cannibals*

homework, so he had come to the fish shop to return the pot as Kotoko-san had asked, but the small old pot, and the time he had spent helping with the beans suddenly all felt like a waste. As he turned to leave Jinko-san said, "Wait."

"I don't need a Coke."

"Mrs. Aida came here to buy something yesterday."

"And?" Toma froze. He felt ashamed.

"You haven't been seeing Chigusa-chan lately?"

"Who cares."

"Aida-san was worried."

Jinko-san's voice was unnecessarily quiet, like she was whispering a secret into his ear. It was the voice of a mother worried about her son. This disgusted Toma.

"It doesn't matter." But he kept speaking. "Chigusa's mom say anything?"

"Hm? Say something? What? ... You never hit Chigusa-chan, right?"

Toma was silent. He could not explain to his mother that he had not hit her, he choked her. Jinko-san picked up her pack of cigarettes as if in a gesture of defeat and said, "You probably weren't ready for it when you hit her, but now you've done it you better get yourself ready. You can't tell what kind of situation you might get into. The first time that happened to me, I genuinely thought I was gonna kill him.

It's still so strange to me. Why didn't I kill him then? And you know what, you know that man's scary eyes, you had the same eyes the other day, that condescending look. He hit me just to make himself feel good, but those eyes, they never laughed at my stump. Never made fun of it. He just hit me."

When Toma left the fish shop he thought to himself, I didn't have a Coke. The woman was back in her usual spot.

When he got home and headed upstairs, Kotoko-san called after him. "Do you have a second?" Her voice was different from usual. It was more formal, as though there was something, somewhere frightening her. She checked the front door and then the back door on the other side of the kitchen before turning her gaze to Toma and bringing her body close to his. It smelt like a rainy night.

"Mā-kun, I've decided to leave. I can't go without telling anyone thank you for everything, so I'm telling you. Just you. Okay?"

"You're not gonna say anything to Dad?"

"Promise you won't say anything until I'm gone? Who knows what he would do. He's hurt me so much, so now, at the end, I at least want to get out without anything happening."

"Um, are you gonna go with the man from the bar?"

"Sadly, no. I'm going by myself. Well …" She rubbed her stomach. "This one won't be any help yet."

*Cannibals*

"Today?"

"No."

"Do you have money."

"That's not for a kid to worry about."

"I'm sorry, I …"

"What?"

"I always thought that Dad was the biggest idiot, but you and Jinko-san were stupid too. Why? Why do women stay with men who hit them? But you're not stupid. You wanted to run away. And I never stopped him, so that makes me an idiot just like him."

"No matter what awful things happen, Mā-kun, you better not call yourself or your parents stupid. If things are that bad, maybe you better start thinking about leaving too."

Even after Toma climbed upstairs, the smell of rain at night stayed with him. If Kotoko-san really left, he could not imagine his father following her. When he wondered if he and Jinko-san would also spend their whole lives in the riverside like his dad, he felt that everything he did was pointless.

He thought of Chigusa. And at the same time, the crushed unagi head popped into his mind.

The town's little shrine did not have its own Shinto priest, so the men of the riverside prepared for the festival on their own every year. Toma also helped, hanging streamers from the willows and telephone poles. In his spare moments between running around to get supplies for the booths, Toma's father would carefully rub Kotoko-san's belly, as though it was the very head of a newborn and talk about the baby. "What should we name it? I think we should give it a one-character name like me this time. Whether it's a boy or a girl."

Toma's name was also given to him by his father.

Kotoko-san did her chores, her face betraying nothing, and went to work. Since she's pregnant with my father's child, maybe she looks sort of like Jinko-san did when she was pregnant with me, Toma thought. Jinko-san stayed in the riverside, but Kotoko-san is trying to leave. And I am no longer in anyone's stomach.

A large snail crawled along the edge of the veranda, exposing itself to the dry air. Toma had no idea why such a creature was out in the sun. He stared at its round shell as it moved. It was neither a dream nor a trick of his vision. Toma thought he might be able to see the time that flows through the riverside and occasionally gets backed up, but no matter the angle, however he looked at it, that snail was in the end nothing more than a shell spiraling to the right, with flesh that was soft but surely tough if you bit into it. One reason he could see the shining ends of its feelers was because of how large the snail was, but it was also because he was so close to it. He could hear his father and Kotoko-san's voices in the distance. The snail looked as though it was entirely oblivious to its surroundings, not even aware of the ledge of the veranda it was crawling along at that very moment. Would he stay in the riverside like Jinko-san, or copy Kotoko-san and leave, how would his father react when he found out Kotoko-san had vanished, when would he be able to meet Chigusa like before and have sex? Toma pondered these questions as he stared at the snail inching along, nothing to do with his concerns.

From the next day, Toma began walking aimlessly along the edge of the river, running up to the shrine, and wandering by Chigusa's house though he knew he would not be able to see her. He continued to masturbate in the bath.

He was not sure exactly how many days had passed. Toma wanted to see a crushed eel head, so one noon he went fishing in front of the fish shop without being commanded to by his father. The red dog was howling. The unagi were not biting. He caught a large prawn that looked hollow as a sloughed off shell, holding firmly on to the worm hanging off the hook. When Toma looked at the water, he realized the tide was so low there was no hope of even catching a small fish. The skull of some sort of animal, which species and where and when it died he did not know, was peeking out from the surface of the mud. It was an old-looking brown that seemed ready to collapse at any moment. Though there had been no rain, the leaves of the willows were a lustrous green. The children that had once mocked him and Chigusa passed in front of the fish shop. Not one of them glanced at Toma. The group squatted down in front of the red dog in unison and took turns petting it. The dog did not resist, laying down on the dirt with its head between its paws, wagging its tail, and rolling over onto its back. Upon seeing its genitals, the children laughed cheerfully. The worms Toma had stashed in the shadows of the hydrangeas to keep out of the sun wriggled their bodies in their jar of dirt. So many were left, maybe he had forgotten to bait his hook. The prawn was hanging on to the hook for dear life. Was it yesterday or the day before that? The woman on the corner in front of the apartment building was laughing. The kumazemi cicada was still clinging to the wall there.

Toma started walking. He was thirsty and his breathing was labored. Sweat got in his eyes. He was being tailed by his own footsteps. When he crossed the bridge, he could swear it was shaking. A heron stood with its legs piercing the riverbed, in its mouth a crab with brown hairs growing on its pincers.

When he arrived at the corner of the apartment building, at first Toma was unsure if he had actually meant to go there, but he was the one who willed himself to stop. The woman was sitting with her cheek resting on her hand. She stood like a bored nurse in a hospital waiting room, seeing a patient for the first time in an eternity.

"Yes," she said. She took Toma's hand, led him around to the other side of the building where the entrance was, and climbed up the iron stairs full of holes from rust.

Realizing that the woman's paleness was really the effect of layers of makeup left Toma in ever greater disbelief of what he was doing. When he undressed her and grabbed her, white stuck to the palms of his hands like peeling, rotten flesh. She was his father's hand-me-down. Even the countless wrinkles folded up behind her ears were painted white. The smell of her body assaulted him. He told himself she was a useless bag of meat. If he convinced himself of that, he thought he would be able to get away from her. But once he thought of her as flesh, his desire burst and his penis grew hard. He tried to think of Chigusa, but it was no use. Without so much as a change of expression on her face, the woman raised her hips and signaled with her body that she was ready to accept him. Toma was overcome with embarrassment and raised his right hand, bringing it down and slapping the woman's cheek. He hit her repeatedly. Each time, she returned her face to its initial position. Her eyes were clear. Her hips were still ready to take him in, and so he did not refuse; he inserted himself all at once and thrust, repeatedly, just like when he slapped her. His torso barely moved as his hips continued to thrust like some machine connected to his body. When he focused on moving his hips, his pleasure increased, and then came a sensation like his hips were beyond his control, moving on their own. The woman's body trembled slightly with the motion of his hips. Her lips were closed tight. He grabbed her hair and twisted her head. He could feel her hair wrapping around his fingers. For some reason he expected her head to come off her body. Bubbles formed at the edges of her tight-pressed lips, and Toma caught a whiff of something like warm excrement. Her eyes rolled back. Her body was ready to snap, but the nipples at the ends of her crumpled breasts were swollen black with confidence; they smacked against Toma's chest, twisted in every direction, and Toma scratched at her scalp with his nails, feeling himself swell to the very brim, and the orgasm struck his body like a hammer. It was his first time without using a condom. He must have gotten it all inside of her. It felt as though he had ejaculated blood. His own blood, as well as the blood of the little brother or sister that Jinko-san never gave birth to, and the blood of his father too. If the woman was a hand-me-down from his father, that would make him the newest father.

When Toma pulled his body away from her, the hairs

*Cannibals*

tangled around his fingers snapped, and the woman for the first time let out a strange whimper.

Looking up, he realized finally that aside from the tatami flooring and walls, a dresser and a refrigerator, there was hardly anything in the room. In the corner of the small sink were the scabbard fish reduced perfectly to mere bones, the heads looking underdone, silver and shining. Toma pulled his clothes on to his sweaty body, checked that the woman was still breathing, and said, "Ask my dad for the money."

The woman spoke, maintaining the composure of a nurse. "I'll give him a good price. You weren't as wild as he is."

He felt the strength drain from his body upon hearing the woman's words. Leaving the room, he realized he had gone through the trouble of arranging his sandals neatly at the dusty entryway. His steps as he descended the stairs rang out loudly and irregularly.

When he reached the riverside road on the back side of the apartment building, there in front of the fish shop on the other side of the river, standing between the two fishing lines still cast into the water, was Jinko-san, looking his way. Jinko-san, who since leaving their home had never crossed and would probably never again cross this river, a mere ten meters wide, was strange to him, just like the sandals he had taken off in the bare entryway.

The reason he found these things, which were not actually strange in themselves, to be so uncanny was because he had no idea how many days had passed since he had watched the snail on the edge of the veranda. It might have been just a few hours. That very moment, the snail was still crawling right in front of his eyes. He thought he may have just been dreaming, but he clearly remembered seeing Jinko-san on the other side of the river when he came from around the apartment building. Holding a fishing pole with her right arm, she flipped it upside down, bringing the reel to the left side, and wound it backwards to reel the line back in. The snail no longer had to bear the burden of the strangeness traveling through the dry air. The sky that had been clear these past days was covered completely in thick sheets of clouds, and the humidity stretched into every corner of the house, like something that had been living there since long, long ago.

Toma got up. His father did not seem to be around. Maybe he was at the woman's apartment. Kotoko-san had not yet vanished and was standing in the kitchen. A sea slater that looked as though it had been washed clean by the ocean tide walked wet and revitalized across the ceiling.

The festival lasted two days; on the first, city councilmembers would give their speeches in front of the shrine, local children who had performed well in kendo or judo or calligraphy contests would be recognized, and then the dancing would begin. This part of the festival had not been around for that long; apparently it had been proposed after the war. They called this one the kids' dance, and it was mostly for elementary and middle schoolers, but adults who liked dancing would join in too. The children came for the sweets and ice cream and plastic models that would be handed out afterwards. The second day was the adult dance. From beginning to end, those of high school age and older danced, the hand motions and footwork of their dance more complicated than those of the kids'. The dancing would stop once, and for about fifteen minutes there would be fireworks which seemed like little more than a practice session for the big fireworks festival the city hosted, and then, after that, the dancing would resume and continue until close to midnight. Toma's father and Jinko-san had first met at this dance. The booths, set up for both days, stretched from the shrine all the way to the river, and in other places as well the residents would set up chairs and benches outside and bring alcohol and the things they bought at the booths. Amidst all that were people who did not contribute anything themselves but walked from house to house eating and drinking, just taking what was on offer. The whole riverside would come to life, and let itself go.

Even though Toma was not sure if he would be able to go to the festival with Chigusa if things continued as they were, he had decided that once it was over everything would be back to how it was before. If he could meet her just once over the two days and have sex, it would be like he had never choked her, and in fact their bond would be even stronger than before they had stopped seeing each other. Though as soon as he found himself thinking this, he realized there was no way things would work out like that. If he were someone like Jinko-san, who prayed at the shrine every day, maybe the festival would have some sort of effect.

As for Kotoko-san, she was her usual self.

Leading up to the first day of the festival, the elementary schoolers gathered to practice their dance in the same shrine grounds that would be the site of their performance. This informal event was itself a sort of ritual, a first sign of the festival's arrival, and the adults who were directing the children were also focused on preparing for the adult dance and making their own plans about where to spend their time drinking after the festivities. The children were intoxicated on this atmosphere so removed from everyday life, produced by the disorganized gathering of grownups caught up in their preparations.

On the evening two days before the festival, Toma wound

up climbing the stone steps to the shrine because of the children who had come calling at his house begging incessantly for him to teach them the dance. The adults had left the middle schoolers to watch over the dance practice and bang the taiko drums and were sitting on the stone platform of the shrine drinking canned beers. The children pulling on Toma's arm were out of breath, their sunburnt cheeks shining. Trying to lead him to an area where there were fewer people, they smiled as they dragged Toma along and wove through the crowd of their friends who had come to the shrine earlier and had already practiced and now wanted to brag about how much they improved. Several faces were peeking out from behind the shrine, and they gestured for the children leading Toma to come. Toma felt the cries of the cicadas were especially dense in that area. He was pulled along further, he was being pushed from behind as well, and when he finally arrived at the back of the shrine, where the sky-piercing, almost black green of the pine grove melted into the green of the hill, there stood Chigusa. They locked eyes. The children took a moment to catch their breath then without saying anything, traded smiles to confirm that their plan had gone as they had hoped, and then one of them, a fifth grader with a shaved head, said, "Mā-kun, you can't just abandon your girlfriend," and ran off to the front of the shrine, the other children chasing after him, occasionally turning around to cast glances at Toma and Chigusa. Though the drums and cicadas were so close to them, it seemed as if the two were left entirely on their own.

"You asked them to do that?" Toma said.

"Why would I? They showed up at my house and told me to come."

"Really? Then why'd you come?"

"Who knows? I didn't know you were gonna be here. But whatever, that's fine. Or what? If you knew I was here, you wouldn't've come?"

"Of course I wouldn't."

"Wow, you don't need to be so sure about it. I wanted to see you."

Chigusa's voice was small, so small it should have been drowned out by the taiko drums, but somehow it melted into the humidity filling the air and rubbed up against Toma's skin. It even felt a little disgusting.

"You remember what I did to you, don't you?"

"If you try to do it again, I'll kill you. Is that good enough for you?"

"Nothing would be good enough. I'll definitely do it again."

"Oh yeah? All you have to do is just not do it."

"That's impossible. I'm my dad's son."

*Cannibals*

When he spoke, he sensed that his voice sounded like his father's and Toma grew afraid; he turned away from Chigusa with violent force, as though he was pulling away at his own face, trying to tear it off. He walked to the front of the shrine without looking back, and the children who had been spying on them surrounded him.

"What's wrong? What'd you do? You're still fighting?"

"Shut up. Mind your own business. Stay away from me."

Toma cut through the ring of children practicing their dance. From the top of the stone steps, the rows of willow trees were hazy with damp. Strangely, despite the sounds of taiko drums and many people talking, a single, clear voice followed after him. He was not hearing it now; it was Chigusa's voice from behind the shrine, when he had turned around and walked away from her. I'll be waiting for you here two days from now. He had definitely heard it. He could not stop moving. The air he inhaled was moist. The stone steps, the path along the river's edge, they were not covered by water, but they were damp. It was not yet raining. A heron puffed up its feathers absent-mindedly as it walked around pecking at the riverbed.

When he returned home, his father's white face was hot with drink. He was laying on his belly on the tatami, his cheek resting on one hand and rubbing Kotoko-san's stomach with the other. When Kotoko-san saw Toma, she said to his father,

"That's enough," and stood up and then said, not directed at either father or son, "Looks like the first day of the festival's gonna be rained out."

His father was still rubbing the air where her stomach once was. "Rain or shine, the festival's the festival. We can't cancel it."

"The weather report says it's gonna be a real downpour."

"We can't cancel for a downpour either. You can't stop the festival for anything. Right Toma?"

Still on his belly, he grabbed Toma's leg. His father's shining pink face was at his feet, softly smiling.

"What're you doing? Let me go."

Toma pulled back his foot, and his father's body rolled across the tatami with a wet sound, laughing from both his nose and mouth. A bag of meat.

In the kitchen, Kotoko-san had begun preparing dinner. She turned towards them and said, "You're both such children."

His father's fingers touched his foot once again, and Toma thought he would hit him.


The next morning, the clouds had come down even lower than the day before, and it felt as though the whole of the riverside had been swallowed up by their damp grayness. It was not raining yet. Upstairs, Toma rolled around, looking at the molding white stains caused by leaks in the ceiling. He prayed, telling himself that if the rain, which was already above the roof and most certainly had no choice but soon, if that rain just did not fall, everything would work out perfectly. He was not sure though what it would mean for it to all work out perfectly. What would wind up how? His situation with Chigusa, with the woman in the apartment, the festival, Jinko-san, the fact that Kotoko-san was apparently leaving, his father. What did he feel, for example, when he thought about his father? How could things work out perfectly with him? Yesterday, he had tried to strike his father. If Kotoko-san was going to leave, did that mean he, who had never once been hit by his father, would face off with him, fight him, and then wind up leaving the riverside like Kotoko-san?

He gripped his penis through his pants. When he thought about how he would no longer be able to see Kotoko-san, he grew hard. Even though he knew he would not be able to see her anymore, he still felt he would be able to keep meeting her for all eternity and have sex with her. Suddenly, the end of his leg felt disgusting to him. The sensation of his father's fingers from yesterday. Automatically, he brushed the top of his foot with the hand he had pressed to his crotch. His foot was wet. The area of the ceiling that leaked had grown slightly darker in color. And as Toma thought to himself, But it's not even raining yet, the next drop fell. He took the washbowl that had been leaning against the wall and placed it in that spot. Then he heard the sound of rain coming from outside.

Just like Kotoko-san had said, it was a real downpour. As night approached, the light faded not to twilight, but to a sickly dimness, and a thin purple darkness that refused to fade fully to black descended upon the riverside. There was no wind. The stench rising from the river filled the air.

From downstairs, Kotoko-san called out, "Mā-kun, I'm heading out." Her voice was the same as always when she went to the bar but clouded with the humidity filling the air. Toma ate alone. The snail on the veranda from some indefinite time in the past crawled up the wooden frame of the shoji.

Toma spent the sleepless night listening to the dripping of the leak. He had switched the washbowl for a bucket before getting into bed so he would not have to empty it in the middle of the night, but by morning even that was full. It looked to Toma like a single, giant raindrop.

His father was not home yet. Kotoko-san, who was also usually back from the bar by now, was not there either. The snail had not moved much. There was still no wind, and the rain fell straight downwards and pounded on the roof. Frogs were croaking in the now flooded garden. When Toma washed his face in the bathroom sink, the tap water, which yesterday ran warm, was cold. He ate the yellow rice left for him in a thermos. It was hard and sticky. After he had finished eating and was washing his bowl, he realized that it was the first time he had cleaned up after breakfast since Kotoko-san had started living with them.

No one returned and there were no phone calls. It would not have surprised him if his father came back, but what if Kotoko-san came back as well? It seemed impossible for Toma and his dad, who should come back, and Kotoko-san, who should not come back, to go on living together. But if Toma was going to leave the riverside, it was no longer possible for him to go with Chigusa. Now that he had known the woman in the apartment, he would hit Chigusa, strangle her. It was funny how little confidence he had that he would be able to have sex with Chigusa without hitting her.

By the time Toma heard the sound of his father's geta signal his return, it was almost noon. He smelled of alcohol. He entered the house with a soft white smile and said, "It's raining, Toma. It's no good. But still, the festival is the festival. Hey, Toma, the other day, you hid from the rain in that apartment, didn't you? Hey? I just wanna say, I'm not mad at you. I'm not mad at all. Good for you. Good for you. You go for it. How was it, hmm? You rough her up a bit too? It was good, yeah? Once you do it once, you can't stop, even if you try. I never tried, though. Oh, and I had a funny idea. Even a monster like that, if you and I keep going at it, maybe she'll have two kids, one for each of us."

After a pause, Toma, looking down at his father sitting on the tatami, said, "How, how you can say that? How can you be like that?"

"Oh geez, that's one tough question. But I guess you know best what's good and what's bad, huh? Maybe you never noticed, but she told me. She told me that when you were pulling her hair and yanking her head around, your eyes were opened wide and your nostrils were all flared out. She said you looked happy as a child."

Toma's father's face was as soft and calm as always. Toma watched as raindrops fell from a space between the veranda and the doorway that had never leaked before. Or maybe there had been a leak there for years.

"You still don't know anything. Kotoko-san, she's never coming back."

Toma surprised himself by saying this. His father stared at him for a moment, then gazed blankly at the kitchen, and then through the open shoji doors in the bedroom, before saying, "And you knew about it, ay?"

"You just never noticed."

*Cannibals*

"So you knew."

"You hit them."

"What?" Toma's father stood up.

"You hit Jinko-san, and Kotoko-san, and the woman in the apartment. How many people did you hit?"

As though he had heard nothing, his father said, "She went and ran with my child." He put on his geta and ran out towards the flooded street.

While Toma grasped in general terms what had just transpired, he could not figure out what he should do. The reason he said that Kotoko-san had run away was because he had wanted to be the one to tell his father, who was oblivious to everything, the truth, but he realized only afterwards that he had also said it because he was jealous of Kotoko-san for so easily escaping from the riverside with only the child in her belly and her own will.

How far had Kotoko-san gotten? The rain was so intense, no matter how she had fled, it would not have been possible for her to have gotten very far in such a short time. His father might be able to catch up with her somewhere. But it would not be right for his dad to return home with Kotoko-san. If neither of them returned, what would happen then?

A new leak opened up in the ceiling, and water ran along the grain of the wood, staining it in long streaks.

After staring at the ceiling for what felt like at least half a day, Toma heard a sound different from the rain, a watery sound like something blowing bubbles, and he went to look at the yard. The earth and rain had mixed together, and emerging from a shallow whirlpool of the resulting mud was a single large unagi with the girth of a grown man's arm, its pectoral fins spread like the cotyledons of a plant, and its head shaking from left to right. There was a wound on its face. At the edge of the wound its smooth flesh glistened, and from it oozed a golden mucus. At first, the eel extended its long body upwards, then fell diagonally, twisted itself, and pulled its body from the whirlpool of mud. It was so big, and it was hurt, but it looked new. For a moment, it stirred up the mud in a single spot, but eventually began swimming slowly away.

Toma sensed something at the doorway, and there were the children, having run there without even umbrellas, standing at attention in a straight line as though they had been handed down orders; they pounced on him. All of them had faces bright red, and steam emanated from the tops of their heads. A tearful voice rose from none of them in particular.

"Mā-kun, the shrine. The shrine!"

"Your father."

"Chigusa."

"We're sorry. We couldn't stop him."


*Cannibals*

By the time Toma had dashed past the neat line of children, he had already remembered Chigusa telling him, I'll be waiting for you here two days from now, but he was not sure how that message was related to what the children were saying.

The road was like a river, and Toma ran pulling his feet from the heavy water with each step. The evening sky was buried in clouds the dull color of yellow earth. He could hear the gurgling of water overflowing from drainpipes and gutters and manholes; the stench of running sewage wafted through the air; mud and stones and potted plants flowed past; rats and insects and frogs all struggled against the water before disappearing in it.

He heard geta splitting through the water and striking the asphalt and saw his father walking, his little remaining hair stuck to his forehead like a baby's.

"Toma, Toooma." His voice had grown childish as well. "I can't find Kotoko anywhere. No matter where I look."

"Where is Chigusa? What happened to her? What did you do at the shrine?"

"Her? I went everywhere looking for Kotoko, and then there by the torii at the shrine was all those kids. They were saying Mā-kun's not here yet, Chigusa-chan's waiting, so I went up to see for myself. She was there. I was looking for Kotoko, Toma. I wanted Kotoko, but you understand, right?

Right, Toma? When you can't hold it back anymore, anyone will do. Any slit will do. Hey, you still never hit that girl."

He spoke as though he was asking if dinner was ready yet, then started walking away. Toma ran in the opposite direction, unable to say anything to his father.

Blue tarps covered the many stalls set up in front of the torii, and there was no sign of any human presence. Toma could feel his feet slipping on the membrane of flowing water that covered the surface of the stone steps. But still he made his way steadily, his feet advancing one step and then another.

The shrine grounds had more or less become a shallow pond. The doors of the shrine were flung open, and inside was a hunched and pale human figure. Toma was frightened; he approached slowly. The corners of Chigusa's mouth were split open, blood was flowing from her nose, and there were fingernail scratches on her cheeks. Her hair stood on end and looked as though it would never return to normal. She was curled up tight, her arms and legs pulled into the center of her torso; her gaze alone extended outward in a straight line. It seemed less like she was looking at something and more like she no longer had the power to move her eyes, leaving her line of sight thus fixed eternally ahead of her. When Toma stepped into the shrine, he was engulfed by the sound of the rain pounding on the roof.

*Cannibals*

"You. It's raining. Why'd you come? With this rain, there's not going to be a festival."

Without moving her eyes, she responded. "I told you I'd be waiting. The kids tried to stop him, but he dragged me in here and locked the doors from the inside. I couldn't do anything. It was over fast, though."

It was strange that Chigusa was talking to him.

"I did this. If I had come, none of this would have happened."

"It's not your fault."

"It's all my fault. I was the one who did this. I did it. I'll kill him."

"Wait."

"Don't try to stop me."

"I won't stop anyone from killing him. But help me. My back is out. I can't stand on my own."

She extended her right arm, which had been wrapped around her body. Toma hesitated but she grabbed on to his hand. She was as cold as ice. Toma squeezed her hand back and helped her up. Chigusa straightened out her knees like a newborn moving them for the first time, carefully checked that each joint moved properly, and then stood solidly on her own feet. They were still holding hands.

"I was so sure I couldn't stand, but I guess I can. Thank you. I won't stop you now."

Toma led Chigusa out of the shrine, and they both got soaked by the rain. When they looked down at the riverside, the lights below were excessively warped. Toma could feel the shuddering of his own body pass to Chigusa through their tightly clasped hands. Chigusa did not tremble.

The water level had risen so much that it was impossible to tell where the river ended and where the street began. The flow of the river was not particularly fast, but the amount of water had increased dramatically, and as the rainwater flowed into the river, in return, the river extended itself, sending water crawling slowly up the road here and there, covering it, and then retracted. A school of goldfish, maybe ones that were supposed to be on offer at one of the booths that night, were swept across the surface of the increasingly indistinguishable mix of rain and river water. Toma felt again and again some unknown creature clinging to and then letting go of his submerged ankles. He was not even sure if they were land animals or ones from the water. His hand was still in Chigusa's. The red dog's barking was not strong enough to be heard through the water, but he still kept it up. A police car was announcing for all to prepare for a flood. In the distance was the sound of geta. Chigusa clung to Toma's arm, and her eyes shone in the rain.

At the fish shop, Jinko-san was bailing out the water that

filled her store. When she saw the two of them, she put down the bucket. It floated slowly on the water. On top of the glass case, which had not a single fish in it, sat the striped cat.

Jinko-san looked at Chigusa's bloody and swollen face, turned to Toma, and said, "That man just came here. He said that Kotoko-san was gone. And he had those eyes again. What did he do?"

"I should have went to the shrine."

"The shrine. At the shrine. He did this at the shrine?" Jinko-san looked at Chigusa again and said, "I should have taken care of him a long time ago."

"I, I will," was all Toma managed to get out before Jinko-san stopped him with the glistening end of her bare right arm.

"You won't be able to. He's never hit you."

Jinko-san took her gaze off Toma and listened. All she should have been able to hear was the rain, but beyond the rain drops that, without striking buildings or the ground, pounded and split the very air itself, she seemed to hear another sound. She scrunched up her face again and again at the barking of the red dog which obstructed her listening.

Finally, by the time she had wrapped the end of her right arm with a towel, stuck it into her prosthetic, which had been hanging on the beam, and tied the belt to secure it, the sound of geta that Jinko-san had somehow been able to make out reached Toma's ears. Chigusa scrunched up her shoulders. Toma pulled her close. The shadow, with a prosthetic for a right hand and a small kitchen knife in the left, said, "You stay here. Protect her." She cut through the water filling the shop and exited. Toma tried to follow her, but Chigusa would not let go of his hand.

"I said I wouldn't try to stop anyone from killing him. I don't care who it is as long as someone does it."

Around them, bugs and spiders floated up, dug out of every crack of the shop by the force of the water, and below them passed the blue-black back of a mullet, long and thin and wedge-shaped. The red dog's barking slipped along the surface of the water and staggered. The striped cat had fallen asleep at some point. The water flowed not in one direction but stalled and made little ripples. And as he identified each of those things, Toma sensed time pass with a frightful certitude. Nothing would now ever return to how it had been. Toma squeezed the hand in his harder and said, "Remember this. I'm a coward. Instead of doing it myself, I'm gonna let my dad and mom kill themselves."

"Is there something wrong with that?"

"Of course there's something wrong with it."

Maybe sensing that Toma's hand would never let hers go, Chigusa softened her grip, as though she felt a little more at ease.

*Cannibals*

The riverside had grown dark. Ceaselessly, time and day-light slipped through the space between raindrops.

Toma noticed on the other side of the river the woman on the corner of the apartment building. She looked like a white flame in the rain. The time he had felt passing stopped, and his slapping that woman, the bubbles she blew out of the corners of her mouth, and the smell of warm excrement all came rushing back to him. A fever rose in his penis, and his grip on Chigusa's hand tightened.

"Ow!"

Upon hearing Chigusa's scream, Toma threw her hand from his own, ran out into the rain, and searched for his father and Jinko-san. Whatever happened, whether he managed to catch either of them or not, it would be better than not chasing after them and hurting Chigusa. The water pulled at his feet, making their movement sluggish. His feet were so heavy he felt they were getting in his way, not the water. He felt as if he was travelling against the flow of time to track down his father and Jinko-san. As if somewhere there was a time when no one hit anyone else and the three of them lived together, properly. Sand and rocks, plants whose roots had let go of the soil and came floating free, garbage bags full of trash, buckets, and shoes struck his legs, tangled around him, and then let go. He was unsure of where he was running, and when he looked to his side, he could not tell the road apart from the river. He continued to advance, knowing that his next step could take him off the road and send him sinking to unknown depths. His intent to run was undermined by his feet growing ever heavier. Soon he realized that on his right, about one meter away, was a row of willows, the tips of their branches floating on the water. Just beyond that was flowing water not the same brown around his feet but a greyish green. What truly surprised him was that there, spanning the width of the river, the water was visibly higher. The green river bulged as big as it could, pressing against both banks, and was pushed back against by the brown flow, and beyond that river, near the bridge, was the faint clomping of geta. Toma stared into the depths of the rain. There, shadows moved, separating into two and coming together into one, but what Toma made out more clearly than those shadows was the sound of his father's deep voice screaming and then, at the end, cracking. And then most clearly of all he heard the *pop* Jinko-san's prosthetic arm made when she removed the rubber stopper before cleaning unagi. The shadows held each other. The rain obscured the bridge, leaving only its silhouette visible directly above the river. He could hear no voices. One shadow parted from the other and then, like the erect stem of an enormous plant snapping under the weight of

*Cannibals*

the rain, slowly tumbled sideways. It stopped for a second as though caught on something, probably the bridge, but soon slipped free and fell into the swollen current of the river. The surface of the river split open just slightly, creating a single wave, but once the shadow was swallowed up, it returned to its original green bulge.

The shadow that remained in the middle of the river walked towards Toma, and right in front of him, it revealed itself to be Jinko-san, saying something. Toma had his hands pressed to his ears and his head facing the ground.

"It's over. Let's go home."

The rain fell on them, and in the dark, Jinko-san's glistening bare right arm seemed skinnier than usual. Jinko-san herself looked stiff and thin. The red stains on her neck and apron had almost entirely been washed away. Suddenly the rain sounded in Toma's ears clearly. The red dog had stopped barking.

They returned to the fish shop, and upon hearing two sets of footsteps in the water, Chigusa came out of hiding from the back. Jinko-san took her place, kneeling up into the room behind the shop, bringing out her cigarettes and lighter, picking up a chair that had fallen over and was half sunk into the water, sitting on it, putting a cigarette to her lips, and dodging the rain drops leaking through the ceiling, lit it, smoked it with ferocious speed, and threw the butt away. "Chigusa-chan, look after this one. You're all safe. You, this one, Kotoko-san, and Kotoko-san's baby, too."

Early the next morning, the police came to the fish shop, where Toma and Chigusa had been sleeping side by side. Jinko-san was not there. The two were taken in separate cars. In front of the shed, the red dog, still chained up, was dead. The sun was out, and the mud covering the road emitted a powerful light. The people of the riverside watched the cars go as they cleaned up after the flood.

According to what Toma heard from the police, since Chigusa had left home and never came back even though it was raining and the festival had been cancelled, her worried parents put in a missing person report, and while the police were searching for her, they had found the body of a dead man in the river. And as for why that led them to search the fish shop, the man, Toma's father, had impaling his stomach something that anyone who lived in the riverside would recognize immediately: the prosthetic hand of the fish shop owner. The body, along with the rubbish that had filled the river, were picked up by the flood and had been flowing to the ocean, but that strange metal tower protruding from him had got caught on the roof of the culvert where the river passes under

*Cannibals*

the highway, so the body was found before it could make it to sea. On its neck and chest were knife wounds.

After stopping at the police station, Chigusa was then taken to the hospital. Jinko-san was found at the shrine grounds not long after the two were taken in. She was sitting at the top of the stone steps, smoking. When she was asked if she was Shinogaki Jinko, she answered, Yes, and then said, It all started when we met at this shrine. After being held at the police station for two days, Toma was sent home.

Wind blew through the riverside, picking up the piles of dirt and clouding the air yellow. The things that had littered the riverbed had been swept away, and in their place new bicycles and umbrellas and buckets, which were of course broken or bent or rusted, had been swept in from somewhere, poking their faces out through the surface of the water and already becoming home to the crabs and sea slaters. Herons alighted on the new earth of the riverside.

The damage from leaks at home was horrible, and the entryway was full of mud. Toma thought about the fact that he would now live there alone, but the idea felt completely unreal. The yard, too, was full of mud and garbage that had been carried in by the flood. He could not find a trace of the whirlpool from which the big unagi had emerged.

The fish shop was also full of mud. When Toma entered,

the striped cat, still curled up on the top of the glass case as if it had not moved since the flood started, jumped down and walked to the rooms at the back of the shop. Toma did not feel the fish shop moved through the cat like he did before; this time, the cat was just walking through the shop. Toma stared for a long while at the beam where, until recently, Jinko-san's prosthetic hand had hung.

Of course the woman was still at the corner of the apartment building. The only thing that had changed about her was that her black hair, which one really could have called grey, had become almost pure white. The red dog's dead body had been cleaned up, and the spot where his empty collar lay was now swarming with flies.

Looking down at the river, Toma thought that if the mud had moved this much, he would probably be unable to catch anything for a while. The fact that even if he could catch another unagi there was now no one to clean it for him was just as unbelievable as the idea of living in that house alone.

The children came running and then stopped some ways off. The little bodies staring at him seemed so sad, so he told them, "You heard about it, right? Yeah, my mom killed my dad. Don't worry. I'm all right."

One of them, the bald headed one, stepped forward and said, "My mom said that the fish shop lady Jinko-san is amazing. After you and Chigusa-chan got taken in, my mom saw her coming down from the shrine with the police. When she got to the bottom of the stairs, Jinko-san didn't walk through the torii, she went around. And my mom said that's cause she's an amazing woman. She said it stopped, but it started again. What's amazing about walking around the torii?"

"You're already in the fifth grade but don't know about the torii?"

Toma's father had been taken to the hospital and then picked up by relatives who held a simple funeral. At the top of his head, above the thin layer of makeup, was hair like a baby's.

Chigusa declined to change schools like her parents had suggested. The scratch marks on her face refused to fade.

"You can do more than look. You can touch them if you want."

Toma had not so much as held her hand since what had happened. He placed a hand to her cheek. He could tell that Chigusa was nervous.

"I guess we won't do it anymore."

"Yeah, that's right."

Her cheek was stiff.

Toma's requests to see Jinko-san were rejected for some time, and he only got permission after a suit was brought. It was already September.

Jinko-san, on the other side of the glass, had not lost a lot of weight. She had looked skinnier on the night of the flood, when she had said, It's over, let's go home.

"This," she said, using her left arm to draw the outline of an invisible prosthetic on her right. "Since I lost it, I feel so much better. I can't clean fish anymore. I guess the shop's time has come."

Toma wanted to say, I'll take over. Just as he finished explaining that he was still going to school and staying at a children's home, their time ran out.

"They said I can bring things in for you if you want. Is there anything you need?"

"Nothing at all."

Toma wondered if the prison provided her with menstrual products.

*Cannibals*

*honfordstar.com*